5/2008

W9-BDP-639

Tales of
Insects

Also by Pleasant DeSpain

THE BOOKS OF NINE LIVES SERIES

The Dancing Turtle
A Folktale from Brazil

The Emerald Lizard
Fifteen Latin American Tales to Tell in English & Spanish

Sweet Land of Story
Thirty-Six American Tales to Tell

Thirty-Three Multicultural Tales to Tell

Eleven Turtle Tales
Adventure Tales from Around the World

THE BOOKS OF NINE LIVES

VOLUME SIX

Tales of Insects

Pleasant DeSpain

Illustrations by Don Bell

August House Publishers, Inc.
ATLANTA

Published 2002 by August House Publishers, Inc.
3500 Piedmont Road, NE, Suite 310, Atlanta, Georgia 30305
404.442.4420
www.augusthouse.com

Printed in the United States of America

10 9 8 7 6 5 4 3 2   HB

LIBRARY OF CONGRESS CATALOGING-IN-PUBLICATION DATA
DeSpain, Pleasant.
  Tales of insects / by Pleasant DeSpain .
    p. cm. — (Books of nine lives ; 6)
  Summary: A collection of nine traditional tales about insects from various
  parts of the world, including Mexico, Japan, Jamaica, and Fiji.
  ISBN-13: 978-0-87483-668-4
  ISBN-10: 0-87483-668-9
  1. Insects—Folklore. 2. Tales. [1. Insects—Folklore. 2. Folklore] I. Title
  PZ8.1.D453 Tak 2002
  398.24'5257—dc21   2002071695

Executive editor: Liz Parkhurst
Text designer: Joy Freeman
Cover and book illustration: Don Bell

The paper used in this publication meets the minimum requirements
of the American National Standard for Information Sciences—
Permanence of Paper for Printed Library Materials, ANSI Z39.48–1984.

AUGUST HOUSE   PUBLISHERS   ATLANTA

For Greg and Juleen Feazell,
my brother and sister-in-law,
with love and appreciation.

Acknowledgments

I'm fortunate to have genuine friends and colleagues without whose help the continuation of this series would not have been possible. Profound thanks to:

- Liz and Ted Parkhurst, Publishers
- Don Bell, Illustrator
- Joy Freeman, Project Editor
- Margaret Read MacDonald, Storyteller, Author, Librarian
- Jennifer D. Murphy, Head of the Children's Department, Albany, New York, Public Library
- Candace E. Deisley, Youth Services Librarian Albany, New York, Public Library
- Denver Public Library
- Lakewood, Colorado, Public Library
- Seattle Public Library
- University of Washington Library (Seattle)

The Books of Nine Lives Series

A good story lives each times it's read and told again. The stories in this series have had many lives over the centuries. My retellings have had several lives in the past twenty-plus years, and I'm pleased to witness their new look and feel. Although *The Books of Nine Lives* series began with a variety of thematically based, and previously published, multicultural tales, all nine of the stories in Volume 6 are printed here for the first time.

This particular series takes on a life of its own with this volume, and the three volumes to follow. They are timeless, ageless, universal, useful, and so-very-human tales that deserve to be read and told again.

I'm profoundly grateful to all the teachers, parents, storytellers, and—most of all—the children who have found these stories worthy of hearing and sharing. One story always leads to the next. As evolving human beings, we are more alike than we are different, each with a story to tell.

—*Pleasant DeSpain*
Troy, New York

Contents

Introduction

Insects are much more than small, invertebrate, cold-blooded animals with segmented bodies, several pairs of legs, and one or two pairs of wings. In story-lore, insects are teachers, friends, tricksters, hard workers, fools, and heroes. Of all the insect tales told during the past several hundred years, the greatest number are told about Spider. Perhaps this is because spiders survive in nature through an unparalleled intelligence and determination. They give as well as take. Their silken webs are both beautiful and deadly. The African trickster, Anansi, is the champion spider, because so many tales are told of his exploits.

I recall hearing "Athena and the Spider" in elementary school. Athena, the daughter of Zeus, was a skillful artisan who wove fine cloth. Upon hearing that a mortal named

Arachne boasted that she was the better weaver, Athena flew into a rage. She turned Arachne into a spider, saying, "With the finest thread, you will weave forever."

From that day in school, so long ago, I saw spiders, and the host of insects, in a different light. They were no longer bugs and worms to be feared or ignored but rather vital and natural creatures who make important contributions to our planetary survival. Stories showed me then, and to this day, a healthier and more interesting way to experience nature.

In this multicultural collection, I've included traditional tales from many countries involving a variety of insects. Here you'll find the Cherokee version of the first fire and the West Indies trickster tale making Granny dance. A grasshopper story originates in Mexico, and an ant tale comes from Burma. Firefly is represented in a Jamaican story, and Fiji's Butterfly gets to show her cleverness. Spider appears in both Japanese and Ashanti tales, and Wasp and Bee tell their Nigerian story.

Read and share these tales again and again. We can learn much from the insects of our world, and story makes a fine teacher.

The First Fire

Cherokee

In the beginning time, there was no fire. Mother Earth was cold. Nighttime and wintertime were filled with dread. The People and the animals suffered.

Rain fell hard from the dark sky one night. Thunder boomed, and lightning struck a hollowed-out sycamore tree on an island. Fire grew in the bottom of the hollow tree. Smoke rose up through its branches, embracing wet clouds.

The animals gathered on the lake shore. "Who will go and get the fire?" they asked each other.

Raven said, "I'll fly across the water to the island. I have strong wings and a sharp beak. I'll bring the fire home."

Raven flapped his wings and flew to the small island in the middle of the lake. He settled on a branch near the top of the smoking sycamore tree. Flames leapt up at Raven and scorched his feathers black. He grew frightened and flew back to the council of animals. His feathers have remained black to this very day.

Hoot Owl said, "I'm not afraid of fire. I'll bring it home."

She flew to the island and sat on the topmost branch of the sycamore tree. The fire burned hotter and leapt higher. A blast of hot air, followed by smoke and ashes, nearly blinded Hoot Owl. It made white rings around her damaged eyes. She returned without fire and has trouble seeing to this day.

"I'm a strong swimmer and a good climber," said Blacksnake. "I'll get fire."

After swimming the long distance to the island, Blacksnake began to climb up the burning tree. Suddenly, a piece of the bark gave way and he fell into the fire at the center of the tree. He escaped the burning flames and returned without fire. This is why Blacksnake is black all over.

The other animals said it was too dangerous to get fire. The other animals said that they didn't want to be burned. The other animals said that they could live without fire, as before, even though it was cold at night.

Water Spider said, "No. We need fire. I'll go."

"You are too small," said Antelope.

"You can't fly," said Eagle.

"You can't swim," said Otter.

"You have no way to carry fire back from

the island," said Fox.

"I'll go," said Water Spider, "and I'll return with fire."

She began to spin a length of silk. She spun and spun until it was long enough to weave into a small bowl. After tying the bowl onto her back, she stepped lightly on the water and raced to the island. The wind blew hard and the fire in the tree began to go out. She quickly grabbed up a small piece of smoldering wood and placed it in the silken bowl.

Water Spider ran back across the top of

the water to the animals waiting on shore. A wisp of smoke rose from the glowing ember. The animals gathered kindling and used the ember to start a fire.

Water Spider brought fire to the animals. The animals gave fire to the People. Now nighttime is bearable, even in the coldest of winters.

Dance, Granny, Dance!

Antilles, West Indies

Granny was an old lady who had dancing feet. When the drums began pounding with a soft, slow beat, Granny moved as smooth as molasses sliding down the side of a jar. When the drums pounded fast and loud like thunder ripping the sky, Granny leaped and twirled like a deer in flight. Granny's old bones had rhythm. Granny's skinny arms had rhythm. Granny's black toes had rhythm.

When the drums sounded, the people gathered to watch, and a chant was heard.

Dance, Granny, dance!
Dance, Granny, dance!
Dance, Granny, dance!

Granny was not only known for her dancing, she was also famous for her garden. She grew the largest, most delicious vegetables on the island. She knew the soil. She knew the seasons. She knew the rain. Everyone wanted Granny's potatoes, corn, beans, and squash. She sold her produce at the Saturday market and always came home with her baskets empty and her purse full.

Anansi, the spider, hearing about Granny's tasty vegetables, decided to pay her a visit. He found her working in the garden.

"Hello, Granny," said Anansi. "My, but it's a hot day."

"Hello back, Mr. Anansi. Yes, it's toasty. Why don't you sit in the shade of that tree, back behind the fence."

"The tree is too far away, Granny, dear. I wouldn't be able to watch you work. You have such a graceful way of moving."

"Aren't you nice? Would you rather grab the hoe and help me weed this patch of garden?"

"No, no, sweet lady. I wouldn't know how to do it. You're the expert at weeding. I'll just sit here and watch. By the way, you grow the most beautiful vegetables I've ever seen."

"Yes, folks around here seem to like what I grow."

"Now Granny, I'm sure that you have more food here than you can eat. Give me the extra bounty, and I'll take it to the poor people on the island."

"Everyone on the island is poor," said Granny, "including me. That's why I sell my vegetables at Saturday Market. You can buy some today if you have money."

Anansi didn't have money. He never paid

for anything. Suddenly he remembered that Granny liked to dance. The spider picked up two strong sticks and began pounding a rhythm on a nearby log. He started slow and steady, steady and slow. Granny's feet began to shuffle among the squash plants, back and forth, forth and back.

He drummed on the log a bit louder, a bit faster. Granny picked up her heels and began to twirl around the edges of the large garden. Around and around she went. Anansi put everything he had into beating the sticks on the log. The steady rhythm ran faster and faster. Granny flew into the air and laughed and danced.

> *Dance, Granny, dance!*
> *Dance, Granny, dance!*
> *Dance, Granny, dance!*

She danced out of the garden and down

the path. She danced to the east and then to the west. She danced to the north and then to the south. She danced all over the island. She danced until the sun began to set. She

danced on home, and to her great surprise, a large basketful of ripe vegetables was missing. So was Anansi.

A few days later, Anansi returned to Granny's garden. She was busy watering plants.

"Hello, Granny, don't you look fine today?"

"Don't hello me, you thief. Where's the money for the vegetables you took?"

"Me, steal from you?"

"You're Anansi," said Granny with a huff. "Everyone knows that you steal."

"Then let me make it up to you, dear lady." He picked up the sticks and began pounding out the rhythm on the log. He drummed soft and slow and loud and fast. He drummed until Granny's feet couldn't stay still. She shuffled and ran and leaped and twirled.

Dance, Granny, dance!
Dance, Granny, dance!
Dance, Granny, dance!

She danced out of the garden and down

the path. She danced to the east and then to the west. She danced to the north and then to the south. She danced all day and into the night. She danced on home. Another basket of vegetables was gone. So was Anansi.

Three days later he returned to the garden. Granny was harvesting beans.

"My dear Granny," he said, "what can I do to help?"

"You can pay me for all the vegetables you've taken."

"You know I have no money. What can I give you instead? How about a nice tune?"

He picked up the sticks and pounded the log.

> *Dance, Granny, dance!*
> *Dance, Granny, dance!*
> *Dance, Granny, dance!*

She danced out of her garden and down

the path. She danced to the east and then to the west. She danced to the north and then to the south. She danced all over the island. She danced until the sun began to set. Once home, she saw that more vegetables had vanished. So had Anansi.

Four times he came and four times she danced. In the end, she didn't mind all that much. To move smooth like molasses and leap high like the deer, to dance the island from end to end, to still feel the rhythm of life in the soles of her old feet, this was her reward. Besides, who ever heard of getting the best of Anansi?

Dance, Granny, dance!
Dance, Granny, dance!
Dance, Granny, dance!

Grasshopper's Army

Mexico

King Lion was taking a siesta one summer afternoon, dreaming of the glories of his youth. Suddenly he was awakened by a loud buzzing in his ear. Using his massive paw to swipe at his ear, he heard a voice: "Watch it! You nearly killed me."

Lion looked about but didn't see anyone. His ear itched and he scratched it with a sharp claw.

"Stop it, I say," came the voice. "I'm not to be trifled with."

"Who are you?" roared Lion. "Where are

you?"

Grasshopper jumped from Lion's ear down to the ground, in a single hop. "I'm here, right in front of you," he chirped.

Lion rubbed his eyes and looked again. "Little Grasshopper. How dare you disturb my nap? I've a good mind to step on you."

"I wouldn't if I were you, King Lion. I'm stronger than I look."

"You, strong? I think not," said Lion. "In fact, I wonder why you even exist. You and your friends are nothing but a nuisance."

"That's not fair," said Grasshopper. "We belong in the world, the same as you."

"You're nothing like me. I rule the animals because I'm powerful and can roar. Burro runs fast and has sharp hoofs. Ox is strong and never backs down from a fight. Fox is clever and doesn't get caught. Panther, Javalina the wild pig, and Coyote are great warriors as well. You, on the other hand, are small and noisy and disturb my sleep. You do not belong here."

Grasshopper was infuriated by Lion's words. "Very well, Your Royal Highness, this means war. Gather your army and prepare to do battle tomorrow. I'll lead my troops to the big meadow down by the river. We'll meet you there when the sun climbs highest."

Lion roared with laughter. "I'm so frightened, Captain Grasshopper. Indeed, we'll have a battle. I look forward to it."

Grasshopper leaped into the tall grass and disappeared from Lion's sight. He contacted his friends and told them to prepare to fight. Red Ant, Hornet, Mosquito, Cricket, and Spider agreed to be soldiers. They also agreed to bring their entire families with them.

Day turned to night, and night back into day. The sun crept slowly to its zenith. Grasshopper was alarmed when he saw

Lion's army all in a row at the far edge of the meadow. The families of Burro, Ox, Panther, Javalina, and Coyote had gathered to fight. They were huge. They were strong. They were fast. They were ready.

Grasshopper's army was prepared as well. Crouched low in the tall meadow grass, they were hard to see. Red Ant, Hornet, Mosquito, Cricket, Spider—and all their family members—waited for the signal to charge. They were small. They were fast. They were survivors. They were ready.

Lion roared. "Grasshopper! Did you bring your army?"

"I did!" chirped Grasshopper. "Are you ready for battle?"

"We are, and may the best army win. That would be us, by the way," bragged Lion.

"We, too, are ready," announced Grasshopper. "May the best army win."

Lion roared, and his troops advanced to

the center of the meadow. Grasshopper blew
a bugle, and his troops raced to meet them.
A large cloud of flying mosquitoes and hor-
nets led the way. The red ants, black crick-
ets, and swift spiders ran across the soft
meadow floor. The fighting began. The stinging, biting, buzzing, and slicing, all weapons
of the insect army, took the beasts by surprise. They cried out—"Ouch! Ouch!
Ouch!"—again and again.

Burro and his family were the first to turn
and flee. Ox and her family were close

behind. Realizing that the battle was lost, the families of Panther, Javalina, and Coyote ran for cover as well. Lion was left alone on the field of battle.

"I give up," he roared. "You have defeated us."

Grasshopper sounded his bugle, and all the fighting ceased. "Do you agree that even though we are small, we deserve a place in the world?"

"I agree," nodded Lion. "You may be small, but you put up a good fight. Now, if you'll allow, it's time for my afternoon siesta."

"I'll join you," said Grasshopper. "All this fighting has made me sleepy."

King Lion and his friends never again doubted the strength of the insects.

Ants Live Everywhere

Burma

Lion, the King of Beasts, ruled the jungle with absolute power. He decided which animals, birds, reptiles, and insects could live in the jungle with him. He also decided which ones had to leave.

Ant loved the jungle. The earthen floor was soft on his feet. The broad green leaves provided him protection from the hot sun and food for his large family. When it rained, as it often did, there were many tall trees to climb to keep from drowning. Ant often said that the jungle was a perfect home.

One day Lion lay on the river bank, basking in the sun. Ant crawled under a nearby leaf. He came to a small hill that was in his way and crawled over it. That was a mistake, as the hill was one of Lion's massive front paws.

"How dare you walk over me, Ant? And without permission of any kind? I am your king and ruler, after all."

Ant was in a hurry to get home to his family. Rather than apologize for his mistake, he said, "It would take me forever to walk all the way around you, King Lion. Besides, I don't weigh much. I'm sure I didn't hurt your paw."

"Enough of your insolence," growled Lion. "I order you and your kind out of my jungle. Find somewhere else to live."

This is terrible, thought Ant. *This is cruel. He can't order us out of our home, not without a fight.*

Ant hid under a nearby leaf until night-fall. He waited until he heard Lion snoring. Carefully he crawled up Lion's body and into his cavernous ear. Ant followed the tunnel down inside Lion's ear and made himself at home. Then he scratched at the sensitive wall of the ear with his long antennae.

Lion mumbled in his sleep and scratched at his floppy ear. It still itched. Suddenly, he heard a tiny voice from inside his head: *Ants live everywhere.*

Lion awoke with a start. "Who said that?"

Parrot squawked in the distance. Monkey

screamed nearby. Lion heard the tiny voice again: *Ants live everywhere.*

Lion shook his massive head, causing his mane to fly. He scratched his ear again. "Who's saying that?" he asked.

You are saying it, came the reply from inside his head. *Ants live everywhere.*

"If I'm saying it, then it must be true. I'm the king, after all." He lay his head on his front paws and went back to sleep.

As soon as Ant heard snoring, he crawled out of the ear and back down Lion's powerful body to the ground. He stayed under a leaf for the rest of the night.

Early the next morning, Lion roared, "Where is Ant? I want to see Ant."

"I'm right here," said Ant, peeking from under the leaf.

"I've changed my mind about where you and your family can live. From now on, ants live everywhere. Is that understood?"

"Yes, and thank you, Your Majesty. You are most wise."

Ant hurried home and told his large family the good news. And that is why, even today, ants live everywhere in the world.

Firefly Lights the Way

Jamaica

Firefly flew through the night sky, blinking her taillight on and off, off and on. She was on her way to the secret valley of fresh eggs, on the island of Jamaica. They were the freshest eggs in the tropics, and she always went on nights when the moon was neither full nor bright.

Firefly had a fine head for the egg business. She always had dozens to sell, and they tasted good. Everyone on the island bought their eggs from Firefly.

Anansi, the spider, went to visit Firefly at

the market. "Tell me, friend, where you find such fine eggs?"

"Since when are you my friend, Anansi?" asked Firefly. "I won't tell you where I get my eggs because you will steal my business."

"Never," said Anansi. "I don't want your business. I simply want to help. Since I'm larger and stronger, I could carry more eggs home for you to sell."

"That would be nice," said Firefly. "What do you want for your help?"

"Six eggs for each trip," he answered. "That's enough to feed my family for a week."

"Very well," agreed Firefly. "Meet me here tonight when the clouds cover the moon. And bring a large sack."

Anansi was happy. Anansi was greedy. Anansi was hungry. Anansi was Anansi, after all. He sewed two large burlap sacks into one huge sack and waited for dark.

Spider waited until the sky glowed deep purple and gray clouds shaded the moon's feeble light. Dragging the burlap sack behind, he ran to the marketplace.

"That's an awfully large sack, Anansi," said Firefly.

"You'll have lots more eggs to sell," he responded with a grin.

"Let's get going. I'll light the way. Be certain to follow close behind."

"I will," said Anansi, "very close behind."

Firefly's tail blinked on and off, off and on, as she flew through the jungle to the secret hiding place. Anansi hurried to stay up with her and was exhausted by the time they arrived. Large, fresh eggs covered the valley floor. All they had to do was pick them up and put them in the bag. Anansi couldn't believe his good fortune.

When the bag was filled, Anansi announced, "Thank you Firefly, for bringing me here. I have enough eggs for my family now. I may even have to sell some of them to my neighbors. I hope you won't mind."

"You said you would help for six eggs. Now you want them all?"

"I'm Anansi," he said. "I can't help myself."

"Then I can't help you get back home. You'll have to do it on your own. It's all a thief deserves."

Firefly turned off her blinking light and flew away.

Anansi had to find his own way home in the dark. He made it out of the secret valley but didn't know which direction to go from there. The heavy sack slowed him down. The wind picked up, and rain started falling. Anansi was tired, wet, and miserable. At last he came to a dark cave and crawled in, out of the storm. Unfortunately, it was Tiger's cave.

"Hello, Anansi," growled Tiger. "What did you bring me tonight?"

Anansi shook with fright. Having tricked Tiger once before, he knew that he was in serious trouble. "Eggs, friend Tiger. Dozens of fresh eggs. I want to make up for the trick I played on you last year."

Tiger tore open the burlap sack and feasted on the eggs. When all but six were devoured, he said, "Wouldn't you like these last few? They are delicious."

Anansi wanted them badly, but he knew that Tiger was testing him. "No, friend Tiger. I brought them all for you. I seek your for-giveness for my foolishness."

"Very well," said Tiger. "I'll enjoy them in the morning. You can sleep in the corner. My snoring won't bother you over there. Good night."

As soon as Anansi crawled away, Tiger slipped a live lobster in the burlap sack among the last of the eggs. Then he went to sleep.

Hearing Tiger's snores, Anansi thought, "Now I can eat." Reaching into the sack, he touched the lobster's claw. It snapped shut, taking a bite from his arm. "Ouch!" Anansi cried.

Tiger awoke. "What's wrong, Anansi?"

"A big flea bit me in my sleep. Sorry to wake you up."

"Think nothing of it," said Tiger with a smile. He soon resumed snoring.

Anansi reached into the sack a second time. "Ouch! Ouch! Ouch!" he cried.

Tiger awoke and asked, "Another flea, Anansi?"

"Yes, Tiger. And he's bigger than the first one."

"If you reach into that sack again, I'll have the flea bite off your hand."

Anansi knew that the game was up and

he was the loser. He ran out of Tiger's cave and hid under a broad green leaf until daylight. The sun showed him the path home.

He tried tricking Firefly into taking him back to the secret valley but never succeeded. Like everyone else on the island, he had to buy eggs from her in the marketplace.

Butterfly's Bet

Fiji

Long-necked Heron stood proudly on his tall, spindly legs, looking out over a calm sea. He liked the sandy shore of this, his favorite lagoon. The round sun was high in the sky. Heron closed his eyes to rest them for a moment.

Suddenly, a slight breeze—like a feather floating on the wind—caressed his forehead and landed on his long bill. He opened one eye and then the other. A large blue and green butterfly stared back at him.

"Remove yourself from my face this

instant," said Heron.

"Excuse me," said Butterfly. "I'm tired from flying all night, and I needed a safe place to land. I didn't think you would mind."

"But I do mind. It's my face, after all. How would you like it if I landed on your face?"

Butterfly laughed. "I doubt that I would mind at all. I'd be dead if you landed anywhere on me."

Heron laughed with Butterfly. "Yes, I'm much larger and stronger."

"You are indeed," agreed Butterfly. "Just look at your long and powerful wings. I'll bet that you would do well in a race to Tonga."

"Tonga? Why would I want to race to the island of Tonga?"

"Because of the beautiful girl-herons of Tonga. Everyone knows about the Tonga herons."

"I haven't heard of them. And I've never been to Tonga. I don't even know how far away it is."

"It isn't too far," said Butterfly. "I could race you there, but I'm a stronger flyer than you are. I'd leave you far behind."

"Don't be silly," said Heron. You are a mere butterfly. I'm a powerful heron, one of the best flyers in Fiji. I would win by a mile."

"Prove it," demanded Butterfly. "I challenge you to a race to Tonga."

"I accept," said Heron.

Excellent, thought Butterfly to herself. *My plan is working. I must get to Tonga today. It's too far away for me to fly there by myself. This is perfect.*

"Ready, go!" cried Heron, flapping his long wings. Up into the air he rose, flying into the sun.

Butterfly hurried to catch up. She flapped her delicate wings as fast as possible and was soon flying neck and neck with Heron, high over the blue sea. Heron flew faster, leaving

Butterfly behind, or so he thought. Butterfly allowed Heron to pass by and settled lightly on top of his back, just behind his head. Resting on Heron's head was far easier than trying to keep up.

Believing that he was winning the race, Heron began to slow down. Butterfly leaped back into the air and was soon head to head with the large bird. Heron was surprised. "Where did you come from?" he asked on the wind.

"I was right behind you all the time," Butterfly answered.

"Not for long," said Heron as he flapped his wings even harder.

Butterfly let him pass by again, and again she settled on his back. And so it went, all the way to the island of Tonga.

As soon as he spied land, Heron flapped his tired wings with the last bit of strength in his body. Butterfly flew back into the air and was soon neck and neck with Heron.

"You are a strong flyer, Butterfly," panted Heron. "I don't think I'll make it. I'm going to fall into the sea."

"I'm exhausted as well," hollered Butterfly. "Let's keep going. Together, we'll make land."

Butterfly, rested from her long rides, led Heron to the island. She slowed down just before landing, allowing the tired bird to win the race.

"If one rides," she said to herself, "one must pay the fare."

The Weaver

Japan

Long ago in Old Japan, there were no fluffy white clouds floating in the blue sky. Clouds did not yet exist anywhere in the heavens. None of the creatures who lived on the earth had ever seen a cloud.

One day, a vegetable farmer named Kobayashi was busy hoeing his large garden. Suddenly a long black snake slithered from under a cabbage plant. Creeping up on a large spider, the snake opened his mouth wide and flickered his tongue. The spider had no chance of escape. Farmer Kobayashi smashed the sharp blade of his hoe into the soft dirt, creating a barrier between snake and spider. The snake hissed loudly, turned around and slithered away. The spider was safe.

Early the following morning, a young woman arrived at Kobayashi's door. "I have no home or family," she said. "I'd like to live here, on your farm. To repay you, I'll weave cloth."

"I have a loom in the spare room at the back of the house. You could stay there."

"Thank you, Farmer Kobayashi. I'll more than pay my way. You'll see."

As the sun began to set in the cloudless sky, the farmer knocked on the door of the back room. The young woman asked him in and showed him the results of her workday. He was astonished. She had woven five long and beautiful pieces of cloth using just a half-bale of cotton. There was enough to make several kimonos.

"How is this possible?" he asked. "You've done an entire week of work in only one day."

"Please, Farmer Kobayashi, never ask how I do it. And please do not come to the weaving room when I'm at work. I'll show you my progress at the end of each day."

She had good reason to ask the farmer to not intrude. For she was the spider saved from the snake. Her intention was to repay Kobayashi for his kind heart and quick thinking. Behind the closed door, she changed herself back into a large spider with eight powerful legs. Digesting the raw cotton, she produced a soft thread from her mouth, just as a spider makes silk for her web. Faster and faster her eight legs flew as she loomed the thread into bolts of fine cloth. All the cotton was used up by week's end.

"I'll go to the village tomorrow and buy

more cotton," said Kobayashi.

The next day, he pushed his heavy cart up the long path to the village market and there bought three more cotton bales. He loaded them in his cart and began the journey home. Halfway there, Kobayashi stopped to rest in the shade of a tree. The long black snake from his garden was sleeping in the grass under that same tree. The snake awoke and quietly slithered inside one of the cotton bales in the farmer's cart.

Kobayashi delivered the cotton to the weaver. She closed the door and, sitting at the wooden loom, transformed herself into a spider. She began devouring the raw cotton. She pulled the thread from her mouth and, spinning the loom faster and faster, wove it into cloth. It was when she reached into the middle of the cotton bale that she screamed!

The snake opened its mouth wide, ready to swallow. The spider leapt out the open window and began running away. The hungry snake followed right behind, gaining ground with each slither. "Help me, Sun in the Sky," she cried. "Please help me."

Sun in the Sky sent a beam of golden light to the earth, and the spider jumped on. Sun in the Sky carried the spider up into the

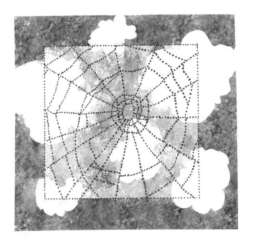

heavens, safe from the snake's reach. The spider was so happy that she began to weave fluffy white clouds from all the cotton she had eaten. She made many beautiful soft clouds, which float about the blue skies to this very day.

Perhaps that is why both spiders and clouds are called *kumo* in Japan.

Wasp and Bee

Nigeria (Yoruba)

In the earliest of times, when God made the world, He decided that a touch of sweetness would be good. Thus he made Bee. Before sending him to earth, God whispered in Bee's ear and told him how to make honey from the nectar of flowers. Bee was a good listener. He heard and remembered everything God said.

God was so pleased with Bee that he made a larger version and called him Wasp.

"Listen closely, Wasp," said God. "I'll tell you everything you need to know about making honey. Honey is one of the sweetest things on earth, and you'll be honored if you learn to do it right."

"Yes, yes," buzzed Wasp. "Please hurry. I'm anxious to get to earth and get started."

God explained all the necessary details, but Wasp didn't listen very closely. He kept flying about God's head, repeating to himself, "I'll show Bee who is the master of honey. I'm bigger and smarter than Bee. That means I'm sweeter."

"Did you understand all my instructions?" asked God. "You seem distracted. Shall I repeat anything for you?"

"No, no," answered Wasp. "I know what to do. Don't worry about a thing. I'll make you proud of me. Wait and see."

God sent Wasp to join Bee on earth.

"I'm already making honey," explained Bee. "The first batch wasn't perfect, but I'm getting better each day. Let me show you

what I've learned."

"You, show me? You, a little bee, show me, a large wasp, how to do something? Stay away from me, Bee, or else."

Bee flew off and left Wasp alone in the big world. Wasp soon discovered a field of wildflowers dripping with nectar. "This should do nicely. I remember God saying something about fragrant flowers."

He gathered as much nectar as he could carry and said, "What's next? Something about a hive and a honeycomb? Which comes first, I wonder?"

Wasp tried and tried to make honey, but all he produced was a poisonous liquid that contained no sweetness. Wasp became irritated, angry, and mean. Wasp began flying through the air, attacking and stinging wherever he went.

Bee continued to learn how to make golden, delicious honey. He became an expert. God was proud of all the sweetness Bee provided for the earth.

God was disappointed with Wasp. This is why Wasp is a noisy enemy who buzzes and darts and stings, producing bitterness in the world.

Why Ants Carry Heavy Loads

West Africa (Ashanti)

Long ago, Anansi tricked Leopard into tying his own tail to a tree. After that, he got Elephant stuck between two strong trees. He even persuaded Python to stretch out and allow himself to be tied to a long pole in order to be measured.

The king became angry at the spider's tricks and decided to punish him. He ordered Anansi to carry a large box. The box was beautiful, but there was just one problem. Anansi couldn't set it down. He tried to set it down, but it wouldn't stay on the ground. It jumped up into the air and landed on his back. Anansi grew tired of carrying the heavy box. It slowed him down and made his back ache. He tried talking to the box.

"Please, Magic Box, get off my back. You are heavy, and I can't carry you any farther."

The box rested quietly upon his back.

"I'll just set you down on the ground for a minute. Would that be all right? Then I'll pick you up again."

The box rested heavily upon his back.

"I have an idea," said Anansi. "I'll set you down and crawl up on top of you. That way you won't get lonely and I'll get to rest. How does that sound?"

The box rested quietly and heavily upon his back.

"No use talking to the box," thought Anansi. "It may be made with magic, but it doesn't listen very well."

Anansi carried the box for several days

and nights. He grew so weary that he couldn't take another step. He lay in the shade of a tree beside the road. Ant walked by.

"Hello, Ant, my friend," called Anansi.

"I'm not your friend," said Ant. "You have tricked me too many times to call me friend."

"I know, and I'm sorry," Anansi replied. "I want to make it up to you. I had this beautiful box made and was bringing it to you. I thought you could give it to your wife."

"It is beautiful," agreed Ant, "but why should I trust you?"

"Because I've carried it so far and I won't set it down, not for one minute. It could get dirty on the ground. You deserve a fine gift after the tricks I've played on you."

"Do you promise that it is just a gift and nothing more?" asked Ant. "If I accept it, you won't ask for it back, will you?"

"I promise, and I promise one hundred times more. I give it freely, and I will never ask you or anyone else to return it."

"Very well," said Ant. "I accept your gift."

Anansi handed the box to Ant, making sure that it didn't touch the ground. Even through the beautiful box was larger than Ant, he was able to balance it on his back.

"I'll carry this home to my wife," said Ant, pleased that he had finally been treated fairly by Spider. "Thank you, Anansi."

"No, no," said Anansi, "I thank you."

Anansi ran on down the road, free of the king's punishment. Ant crawled home with his heavy load and handed it to his wife. When she tried to put it down on the ground, it leapt up onto her back. She handed it to her daughter. The daughter carried it for awhile and then handed it to her brother.

And so it has gone ever since. Ants carry heavy loads—often larger than themselves—

and never put them down on the ground.
When they get tired and need to rest, they
hand it to someone else. All because of
Anansi.

Notes

The stories in this collection are my retellings of tales from throughout the world. They have come to me from oral and written sources and result from thirty years of my telling them aloud.

Motifs given are from *The Storyteller's Sourcebook: A Subject, Title and Motif Index to Folklore Collections for Children* by Margaret Read MacDonald (Detroit: Neal-Schuman/Gale, 1982).

The First Fire — Cherokee

Motif A1415.2.3. The origin of the initial written version of this story is clear. In the summer of 1887, a twenty-four-year-old white man named James Mooney journeyed into the back country of North Carolina to study the language and lore of the Cherokee Nation. His interpreter on the Qualla reservation was a young Cherokee named Will West Long. With Long's help, Mooney was able to record myths and tales born and nurtured in the Cherokee oral traditions. He published the results in *The Myths of the Cherokee, 19th Annual Report of the Bureau of American Ethnology, 1900.* This story is found in Part 1: pp. 240-242. This information is provided in

Cherokee Animal Tales by George F. Scheer (New York: Holiday House, 1968), pp. 18-20.

Two variants are found in *Indian Legends Retold* by Elaine Goodale Eastman (Boston: Little, Brown, 1928), pp.25-27; and *How The People Sang the Mountains Up* by Maria Leach (New York: Viking, 1967), pp. 49-51.

Dance, Granny, Dance! — Antilles, West Indies

Motif D2174.2. My initial encounter with this energetic tale was on the island of St. Thomas, at The College of the Virgin Islands, during the summer of 1967. I taught speech, English, and voice and diction. One assignment was to tell a story. Two students, each from different islands, shared versions as told by family members.

I've traced it back to a brief variant found in *Folk-Lore of the Antilles: French and English, Part II,* by Elise Clews Parsons (New York: American Folk-Lore Society, 1936), pp. 314-315.

A lengthy and well-written variant is found in *The Dancing Granny* by Ashley Bryan (New York: Atheneum, 1977).

Grasshopper's Army — Mexico

Motif B263.9. I heard this story during my first lengthy journey throughout Mexico in 1970, from my first English student, eighteen-year-old Jorge, resident of Oaxaca, the Spanish-built city of narrow streets. I asked Jorge how King Lion made it to Mexico. His response was that he must have escaped from the zoo.

A variant is found in *The Buried Treasure and Other Picture Tales* by Eulalie Steinmetz Ross (New York: Lippincott, 1958), pp. 95-102. She selected it from *Picture Tales From Mexico* by Dan Storm (New York: Lippincott, 1941).

Ants Live Everywhere — Burma

Motif A2434.1.4.1 I first heard this story aboard a cruise ship sailing from Darwin, Australia, to Bali, Indonesia, in 1999. As the ship's official storyteller, I told tales and taught writing workshops to twelve hundred educated adults whose average age was sixty-five. These life-experienced and well-traveled students had a wealth of stories to share, both true and traditional. A Thai woman of age, called Nana, told this Burmese tale.

A variant is found in *How The People Sang the Mountains Up* by Maria Leach (New York: Viking, 1967), pp. 105-106. She discovered it in *Bamboo, Lotus, and Palm* by E.D. Edwards, p. 252, citing Sir J. G. Scott: *The Burman, His Life and Notions,* 2 volumes (London: Macmillan), 1882.

Firefly Lights the Way — Jamaica

Motif Q272.5. This story is a delight to share, because Anansi finally suffers a loss in his trickster ways. I first heard this tale in the summer of 1967 while teaching at The College of the Virgin Islands, on St. Thomas.

A variant is found in *West Indian Folk-Tales* by Philip Sherlock (New York: Walck, 1966), pp.97-104. He drew on the collection *Jamaican Song and Story* by Walter Jekyll and David Nutt (London: English Folklore Society, 1907).

Butterfly's Bet — Fiji

Motif K25.1.1. I admit to having taken poetic and storyteller's license with this tale. In the first printed version I encountered, the butterfly and heron both fall into the sea and drown, as Tonga is simply too far away. It was a bad bet for both. I allow them to live.

I discovered it in *Animal Folk-Tales Around the World* by Kathleen Arnott (New York: Walck, 1970), pp. 161-165. She discovered it in *At Home in Fiji* by C.F. Gordon Cumming (Edinburgh: Wm. Blackwood and Sons, 1882).

A Scottish variant is found in *Twenty-Five Fables* by Norah Montgomerie (New York: Abelard-Schuman, 1961), pp. 54-55.

The Weaver—Japan

Motif A1133.5 and B652.2.1. I've long been inter-
ested in multicultural spider-as-weaver tales. It goes
back to hearing a chilling version of "Athena and the
Spider" in childhood. Arachne, the proud mortal,
heartbroken that Athena has destroyed her work,
hangs herself from an oak tree. Athena transforms
Arachne's lifeless body into a spider.

I first heard this Japanese variant at a county fair
in King County, Washington, in 1975. A Japanese
woman, demonstrating the art and craft of weaving,
told the story as she worked.

A variant is found in *Japanese Children's Favorite
Stories* by Florence Sakade (Rutland, Vermont: Tuttle,
1958), pp. 59-65.

For a West African variant, see *Tales From the
Story Hat* by Verna Aardema (New York: Coward,
McCann & Geoghegan, 1960), pp. 20-23.

Wasp and Bee—Nigeria (Yoruba)

Motif A2813. Storytelling within the Yoruba cul-
ture is usually done after supper, when young adult
males gather on doorsteps. After a few riddles are
asked and answered, indicating that the group is
alert, didactic tales are shared.

I heard this story in 1994, while flying from
Seattle, Washington, to San Jose, Costa Rica. My

seatmate, a Nigerian named Basam, heard it as a child.

A printed version is found in *Nigerian Folk Tales* by Barbara K. and Warren S. Walker (New York: Archon, 1980), p. 94. It was told to them by Mr. Omotayo Adu, a Nigerian student from Yoruba, who heard it during his childhood.

Why Ants Carry Heavy Loads — West Africa (Ashanti)

Motif A2243.1. I discovered this tale in *West African Folk-Tales* by W.H. Barker and Cecilia Sinclair (London: George G. Harrap, 1917), pp. 63-67. They heard it from students at the first government-sponsored Training Institution for Teachers at Accra. Many of the West African tales involve Anansi, due perhaps to the abundance of spiders found in dwellings and in nature. Mine is a briefer, less violent rendition that works well with children of all ages.

An even simpler variant is found in *How the People Sang the Mountains Up* by Maria Leach (New York: Viking, 1967), p. 107.